BLOOD ROSES

Wounds and Wings

*A*udrey found him by the side of the road after his girlfriend had left him. The wings were torn off at the shoulder but they were perfectly intact. There was blood only at the place they had been. She put him in her mother's SUV and took him home.

She cleaned and bandaged his wounds. She had never seen anyone's eyes look so sad. The sadness was not hidden by anger or pride or fear; it was just raw sadness.

She gave him some chocolate chip cookies she had made but he only looked at them as if they were bad art. She washed his bloody clothes and let him sleep on her bed with the down quilt covered in pink roses while she slept on the futon. At night he growled in his sleep, gnashed his teeth and threw the rose-covered pillows off the bed.

She decided to call him Sad Lincoln because of his long, sad face and his long, thin body. She went to a thrift store and bought him some thermal long-sleeved shirts and flannel shirts and baggy corduroy pants with the pile only slightly worn down at the knees. The black lace-up boots he had been wearing when she found him on the side of the road were still good but the T-shirt was bloodied and besides he no longer needed the holes ripped out on either shoulder for the wings.

He went for days without eating and then wolfed down waffles and scrambled eggs, potato salad and cheese sandwiches, grilled chicken, steamed broccoli and pie. He surfed the internet and downloaded music that he played for Audrey when she got home from school. It was usually apocalypse rock, grim and sexy. He also liked to design logos with her graphics program and look up websites that dealt with supernatural phenomena. He kept her room clean, fixed her computer and did her chores for her in secret while her parents were at work. Sometimes when she found him at the computer, he was wearing her clothes— her beads and scarves and sweatshirts. Once she woke up in the middle of the night and saw him sitting at her bedside watching her face.

The wounds on his shoulders healed without stitches, leaving scars she longed, but didn't dare, to touch. Except for the time she had tended his wounds she never touched him. Once he brushed against her and she started crying uncontrollably and for no apparent reason. After that he was extra careful and she had no words to explain why she wanted to cry like that again.

She kept him hidden in her room all day, and at night, when her parents were asleep, she took him outside. He told her stories about himself. He told her about the lands where he and his brother ate fruit off the trees and slid naked down waterfalls. He told about his mother who looked like "that actress. Who is that actress?" when he saw *Breakfast at*

Tiffany's with her and she said, "Audrey Hepburn?" and he said, "She has your name? Cool! Yes, her. She looked like that!" and about his stern father with the single eyebrow like his own who ate the marrow from the ox bones and soup made of chicken feet and didn't understand how doing art could be anyone's actual paid work.

Lincoln didn't say much about the girl-friend ("her," "she," as if it were unbearable to say her name), the one who had torn off his wings with her bare hands. Audrey wanted to know her name and see a picture of her but then she didn't. She imagined that the girlfriend looked like the model in the catalogue that she found him gazing at one day, the woman with the cropped platinum hair, the round, dimple-smile face, bronzed, glimmering skin and supernaturally green eyes. He quickly made a comment about how Audrey would look cute in those platforms ("big shoes" he called them), as if he didn't want to hurt her feelings by staring at models. It was scary to realize that he might care that much about her feelings. Who was he anyway? It could never work out. She had found him at the side of the road! He never left her house! He had wings! Well, once he had wings.

She didn't ask him about the wings, because she sensed he was self-conscious about them. It would have been like asking someone about their pimples, even though she thought the wings, and the scars from where the wings were, were beautiful. She did wonder about them, though. She wondered how they got there. She wondered if his mother had

Wounds and Wings

them, if "she" had them. One night when they
were sitting in the garden listening to the
summer crickets and the sprinklers tossing
wet glitter in the moonlight, he told her that
he was embarrassed when he was in high
school. She asked why and he said, "Well,
you know, how teenagers are always embarrassed. You've got zits, greasy hair, too much
hair, whatever." (Now he had dreadlocks as if
in defiance.) That was all he said but somehow she understood that he was referring to
the wings and that they had not been something that anyone else had in the place he
came from, wherever that was.

Audrey had painful, ugly cystic acne when
she was fourteen but her mom took her to a
good dermatologist who gave her a really
strong medication with pictures of deformed

babies on the seal of each pill. Now her skin was clear, so it was worth it. She only had a couple of scars. One was by her mouth and she wondered if it would bother the first boy she kissed. She planned on getting a laser peel when she was older. There were also some studies linking the drug to depression but Audrey wondered how you could tell, when people with acne tended to be depressed anyway.

When she was thirteen, Audrey's mother came into the bathroom while she was in the tub and said, "Oh, your little mound of Venus is sprouting," and it made Audrey so sick that she wanted to throw up all over her mother. She wondered if he had been born with the wings or if they had sprouted during his adolescence, if it had hurt as well as frightened him and if he was grateful to the girlfriend on some level for ripping them off. It was one thing to have hair and pimples but they were normal, they were what everyone had and so it was much less disturbing than growing something completely foreign.

Audrey's period did not delight her either. She found it shocking and, frankly, humiliating to have blood coming out of her vagina. What if she bled through her clothes in public? She'd seen a girl once with a red stain on her white lace skirt and everyone laughed. She imagined that Lincoln would understand this sense of shame, about something taboo but secretly beautiful and empowering, better than most boys because of the wings.

Audrey had a relatively sane mother and father who loved her. She had a nice house to live in and food to eat and cute clothes to wear. She was not exceptional looking but she was pretty enough now that her skin had cleared up and she had what people might call a pleasant if slightly gummy smile, a chic, short, layered hairstyle and a slim body that she liked to dress up in vintage dresses and cowboy boots. She didn't have too many friends, but that was okay; she had books and DVDs and she did well in school and now she had Lincoln. It didn't make that much sense that she felt as wounded as she did.

But she realized that even wounds were okay because maybe the wounds were why she and Lincoln had found each other.

Lincoln eventually got a job designing and managing websites and doing some graphic art gigs on the side, all from Audrey's bedroom. He gave Audrey money for groceries and flowers and marijuana and big shoes. He still never left the house but she had to go to school every day. She applied to a local junior college, in spite of the fact that her parents wanted her to go to an Ivy League school, so she could live at home and be with him.

She missed Lincoln so much during the times she was away that her saliva dried up and her stomach clenched emptily. It was always a relief when she came home to him. Like water or food. Like music or that moment when you cut yourself with a knife and squeeze the skin and no blood oozes out.

Changelings

*H*e didn't see Daisy at first. Not until his dad died of a brain tumor and his girl-friend, Natasha, was killed in a car accident six months after that.

Daisy told him later, "Your brain can only see what it believes is real, Kissy Face. I was here all along."

She had long, wild hair that always seemed to be tangled up with leaves and sticky buds and she rode around on a skateboard as if it were the marker on the Ouija board she kept in her enormous backpack. She wore little kids' faded T-shirts from the thrift shop. One was a green Hulk shirt; one pale pink one with two people silhouetted on a beach said "Rio de Janeiro, Brazil: Land of Lovers." She had a *Wizard of Oz* T-shirt and a hot pink one that said "The Ramones" with all of their names in a circle. "Johnny Joey Dee Dee Tommy." With the T-shirts she wore black miniskirts and black boots and black tights cut off at the feet so they were always running up her leg in revealing, shredded strips like ladders. Her eyes changed color every day.

His dad had the headaches and then they were all sitting in the living room and his mom was crying and his dad was saying words but the boy didn't really hear him. Except he got that his dad had a mass in his brain and would die within the year. Cancer was something all of their brains understood. It was part of their history and you heard about it all the time on TV.

His mom and dad were best friends. They almost never saw anyone else. He couldn't imagine his mom without his dad. They were like one entity. Their idea of a big night was cooking a gourmet meal together (something with figs, something with polenta, pomegranate seeds, salmon), drinking a glass of wine and getting in bed by nine. They had not slept apart one night since they got married twenty-two years ago.

The tumor was inoperable and his dad died faster than even the doctors predicted. His mom became a zombie after that. (His brain knew and recognized zombies from watching old horror movies.)

Natasha had straight, long, brown hair and wide-apart green eyes that were just flooded with light. She always wore moss green Puma sneakers and baggy clothes as if she were trying to hide her beauty, which of course made her seem even more beautiful. She might not have even noticed him if his dad hadn't died, so it was his loss that woke her up just as the loss of Natasha woke him up to see Daisy.

Natasha started emailing him and then they went to the mall and saw *Pan's Labyrinth* and ate a burrito at the Mexican place and avocado roll sushi at the Japanese place and soft-serve ice cream. Natasha reminded him of a cat with her eyes, shiny hair and graceful body.

She had freckles and a merry, slightly manic
giggle. She was a ballerina and always walked
with her toes out. These are the things he
learned on their mall date: Her favorite food
was waffles with whipped cream and strawber-
ries. Her favorite book was called *The Fairies*
and had girls dressed up in wings pho-
tographed as if they were the real thing.
Natasha believed in fairies with a conviction
that did not match her usual laid-back man-
ner. Her eyes would light up even more than
usual and she would talk about them breath-
lessly and with longing, though she had a
superstition about not calling them by name.

Once she grabbed his arm so hard it hurt.

"She's one!" Natasha whispered.

"Ouch! What?"

"One of *them*!"

"What? Who? Ouch, Tash." He didn't see who she was pointing at.

"You only see them if your brain believes they are there," she said, a bit impatiently. "But I never thought they rode skateboards!"

Later, he thought she must have been talking about Daisy, of course.

He believed in death because he had grown up watching it on TV and then his dad had died and that made it really real. He believed in Natasha's death in a car accident with a drunk driver at the ski resort she was visiting with her family because he had never fully believed that she was his girlfriend to begin with. He knew that Natasha's death was real, but he could not accept it. He thought about her all the time. He listened to the Tori Amos CD she had burned for him. He read her books and her journal. Her mother had given him the journal. Natasha mentioned him casually, describing where they went and what they saw. She called him cute once. She said she felt sorry for him. He imagined that her mother had not read that part carefully, or she would probably not have given him the journal, would she? In Natasha's journal, also, was an elaborate description of what "they" were.

"They were earth spirits, part of nature. Elementals. So beautiful! But they were attacked by evil forces and retreated underground. They got sick and skinny. Some people say reptilian. A few of them tried to rescue their children from their own fate. They bravely ventured up above ground and left their babies in baskets on strangers' doorsteps, hoping for the best."

This is what he learned from Natasha and it is what Daisy explained to him as well. In fact, she had been one of those babies. Her parents had discovered her in a basket and called the authorities. Eventually they had chosen to adopt her. But they had no clue as to who she was. Daisy had a plan. She wanted to go find her true parents in their underground lair.

He said he would go with her. He would have done anything she asked him, of course. By then, he was in love with her. She had come to him in his greatest pain and loneliness; in fact, without his pain and loneliness, he knew she would never have come.

"I'm so fucked up," he had told her. "I'm depressed. I don't care about anything. I have ADD. I get bad grades. Even before my dad got sick I was fucked up."

He had never said these things to Natasha. He had not believed she would understand. He had believed she was going to leave him somehow, although he hadn't imagined it in the way it had happened.

Daisy said, "You are not fucked up, Yummy. Your world is fucked up. It is very fucked up. It is a very, very fuckity uppity world and you are just responding normally to its psychotic vibe. Do you hear me? Because this is very important. This is something you need to know in order to change."

"Where do you come from?" he asked in amazement, touching the twigs in her hair.

"From underground, Panda Bear," she said.

❧

The catacombs twisted beneath the canyon. Old stone rooms and tunnels. It smelled of mold and damp earth and worms. He followed her, the circle of her flashlight illuminating the turns in the passage.

They could hear music coming from up ahead, drums and flutes.

The passage opened out into a larger room. The people were gathered around in a circle of candlelight. One woman sat on a large chair made of stones and tree branches. She had branches in her hair like antlers and a dress of torn lace.

"That's the queen," Daisy said.

The queen grinned, baring her missing front teeth. She was a very thin creature with a long, bony face and glittery candle eyes. Next to her was, he supposed, the king. The king looked like a junkie rock star, sinewy with thin, straight pale hair and deep lines in his

face. He had pockmarked cheeks with high
bones, round, sensitive-looking nostrils and
exaggerated lips. He wore an overcoat and
large black boots without any laces. The king
grinned, too.

The people gathered around. They put
their frail, cold hands on the boy and on Daisy.
Their skin reminded him of a snake he had
once touched.

"Stay with us," they said.

"I have to go ask my mom," he said.

"She can come, too. Stay with us. We are
prepared. There will be a revolution. Things
are changing. You just must believe it, yes? You
just must believe."

❧

The boy went back to talk to his mother. She
was sitting in front of the television eating

microwaved frozen pot stickers and a carton of
Ben and Jerry's. He turned off the TV.

"Are you okay?"

She blinked at him, blotting the grease on
her lips with a napkin. "Yes. Fine. And you?
Did you eat? There's frozen mac and cheese. I
was watching *Project Runway*."

"I know, Mom. It's important. I have things
I wanted to tell you.

"I want to take you someplace. Underground. There's a girl I met. She's not from
here. Her real family lives underground, under
Laurel Canyon. They are like this different
race. But they are cool. They want me to stay
with them. I thought you might want to come.
It doesn't seem good for you here anymore,
without Dad?"

She blinked at him. Her eyes were red.

"Heidi Klum is so pretty, don't you think?" she said. "I wonder if that scar her husband has bothers her?"

He went outside. The night air felt damp on his skin. He could smell the tinge of meaty dinners and fireplaces. Some people already had put a ring of ghosts made from sheets and broomsticks around their tree and there were uncarved pumpkins on porches. Daisy had said they could be goblins on Halloween.

"What does a goblin look like, exactly?" he asked.

"A fairy who has lived underground too long. A corrupt-looking fairy."

"I can't dress up like a fairy," he said. "I mean, that word, you know?"

"I know. That's messed up. That we can't use that word. How is eldritch? Is that better?

More manly? Anyway, Toughy, you get to change out of that same flannel shirt and those cords and be a goblin. Goblins are cool."

He wondered if they had Hershey bars underground. If they carved out pumpkins, scooping out gobs of stringy insides and seeds with their bare hands before putting the candles in. Could he listen to his iPod? He wondered if he could stay with Daisy, sleep in the same bed with her. Were there rules about things like that? He had not been inside of her yet but she had gone down on him and swallowed his come in her mouth. When he had reached inside her black stockings she was wet and slippery and she smelled like the flowers at Natasha's funeral.

She called him different names in between kisses. "Cosmonaut. Smooshy. Mister. Mister

Slick. Creamsicle."

He did not think that there was anything wrong with him. That he was delusional or psychotic or even depressed. The world is fucked up, he thought to himself. He cried a lot now. Daisy told him it was a good thing.

"Let the pain wash over you," she said. "Let the pain teach you. If you can feel it then you can feel joy again, Candy Bar. I mean, Manly Candy Bar. You are a very manly candy bar. Real men cry, you know."

He realized how much he had changed.